GOLD FEVER

VERLA KAY

ILLUSTRATIONS BY S. D. SCHINDLER

PUFFIN BOOKS

AUTHOR'S NOTE

GOLD! Word got out in 1849 that this precious yellow metal had been found, and the fever that gripped the world was so intense that California became a bustling state just one year later. During the first five years of the Gold Rush, 150,000 people moved to California, and most of them were miners. They dug their way through the state, tossing up ramshackle mining towns wherever there were reports of a good find. Then, when the gold played out, the miners deserted the towns just as quickly, leaving hundreds of ghost towns behind.

PUFFIN BOOKS
Published by Penguin Group
Penguin Young Readers Group,
345 Hudson Street, New York, New York 10014, U.S.A.
Penguin Books Ltd, 80 Strand, London WC2R ORL, England
Penguin Books Australia Ltd, 250 Camberwell Road, Camberwell, Victoria 3124, Australia
Penguin Books Canada Ltd, 10 Alcorn Avenue, Toronto, Ontario, Canada M4V 3B2
Penguin Books (N.Z.) Ltd, 182-190 Wairau Road, Auckland 10, New Zealand

First published in the United States of America by G. P. Putnam's Sons,
a division of Penguin Putnam Books for Young Readers, 1999
Published by Puffin Books, a division of Penguin Young Readers Group, 2003

1 3 5 7 9 10 8 6 4 2

Text copyright © Verla Kay Bradley, 1999
Illustrations copyright © S. D. Schindler, 1999

Text set in Cheltenham
All rights reserved

THE LIBRARY OF CONGRESS HAS CATALOGED THE G.P. PUTNAM'S SONS EDITION AS FOLLOWS:
Kay, Verla. Gold Fever / Verla Kay; illustrated by S. D. Schindler.   p.   cm.
Summary: In this brief rhyming story set during the gold rush, Jasper leaves
his family and farm to pursue his dream of finding gold.
[1. Gold mines and mining—Fiction. 2. West (U.S.)—Fiction. 3. Stories in rhyme.]
I. Schindler, S. D., ill. II. Title. PZ8.3.K225Go   1999
[E]—dc21   97-49634   CIP   AC   ISBN 0-399-23027-0

Puffin Books ISBN 0-14-250183-2

Printed in the United States of America

For my loving and supportive husband, Terry,
whose grimy, grinning face greeted and
inspired me every time he returned home
from a gold-panning expedition —V. K.

Dashing westward,
Many miners.
Townsfolk snicker,
"Forty-niners."

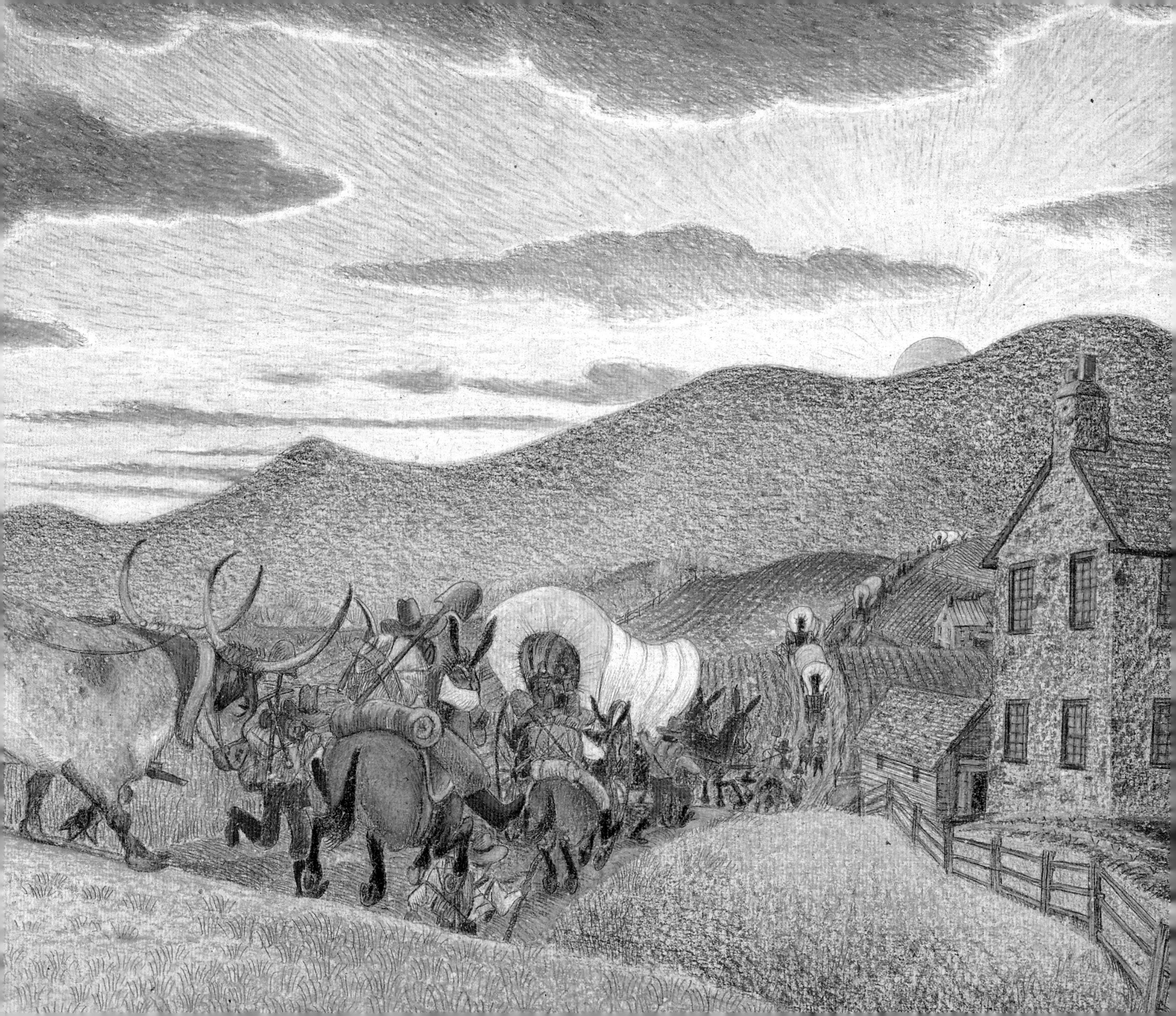

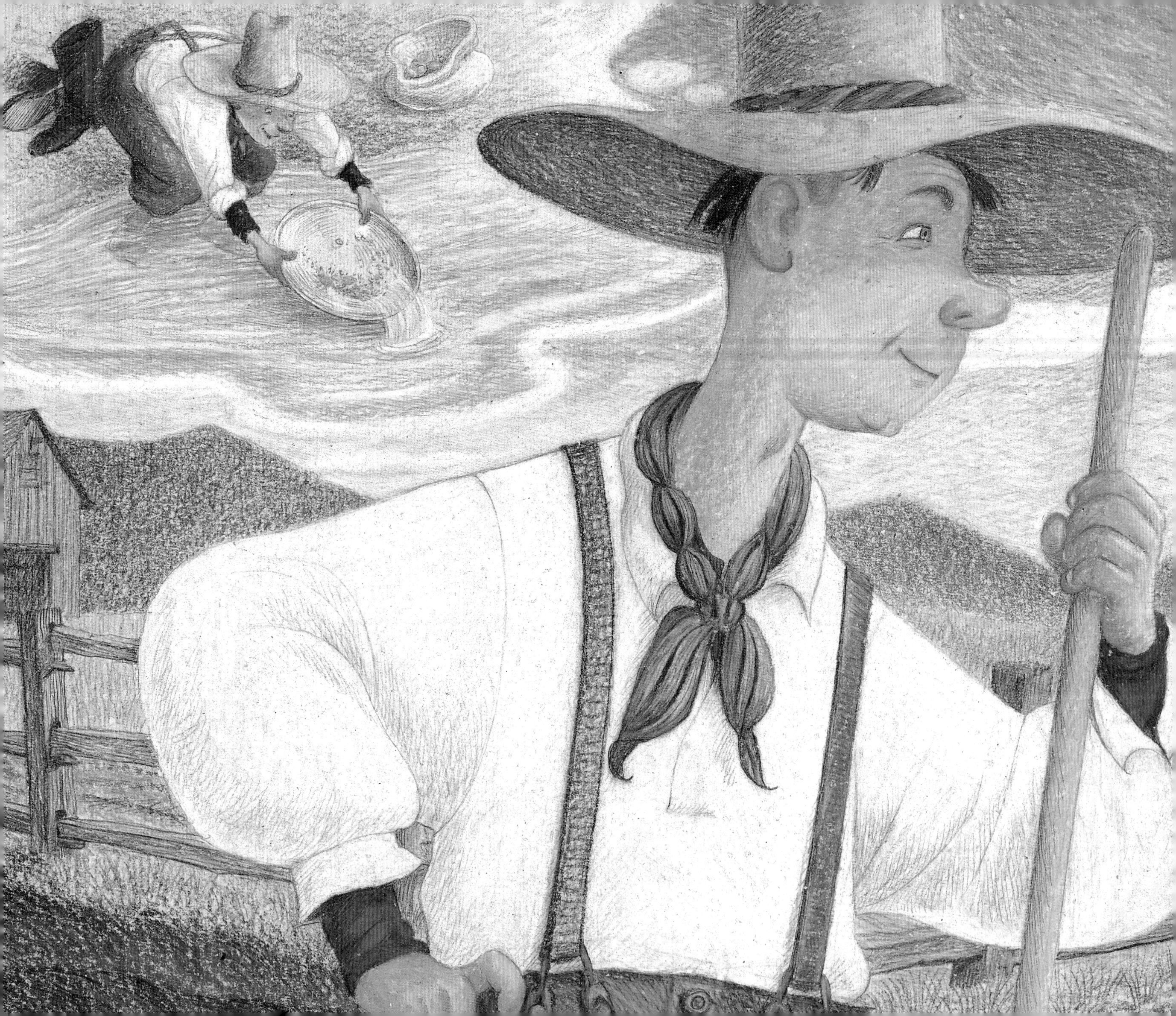

Jasper sighing,
Dreaming dreams:
"GOLD! There's *gold*
In them thar streams."

Packed a shovel,
Pistol, pick,
Goldpan, bedroll,
Walking stick.

No more barnyard,
Pitchfork, hoe,
Farmhouse, family,
"Got to go."

Prairie—dust storm,
River, rocks.

Desert, sagebrush,
Holes in socks.

Vultures, bleached bones,
Craggy knoll.
Empty canteen,
Water hole!

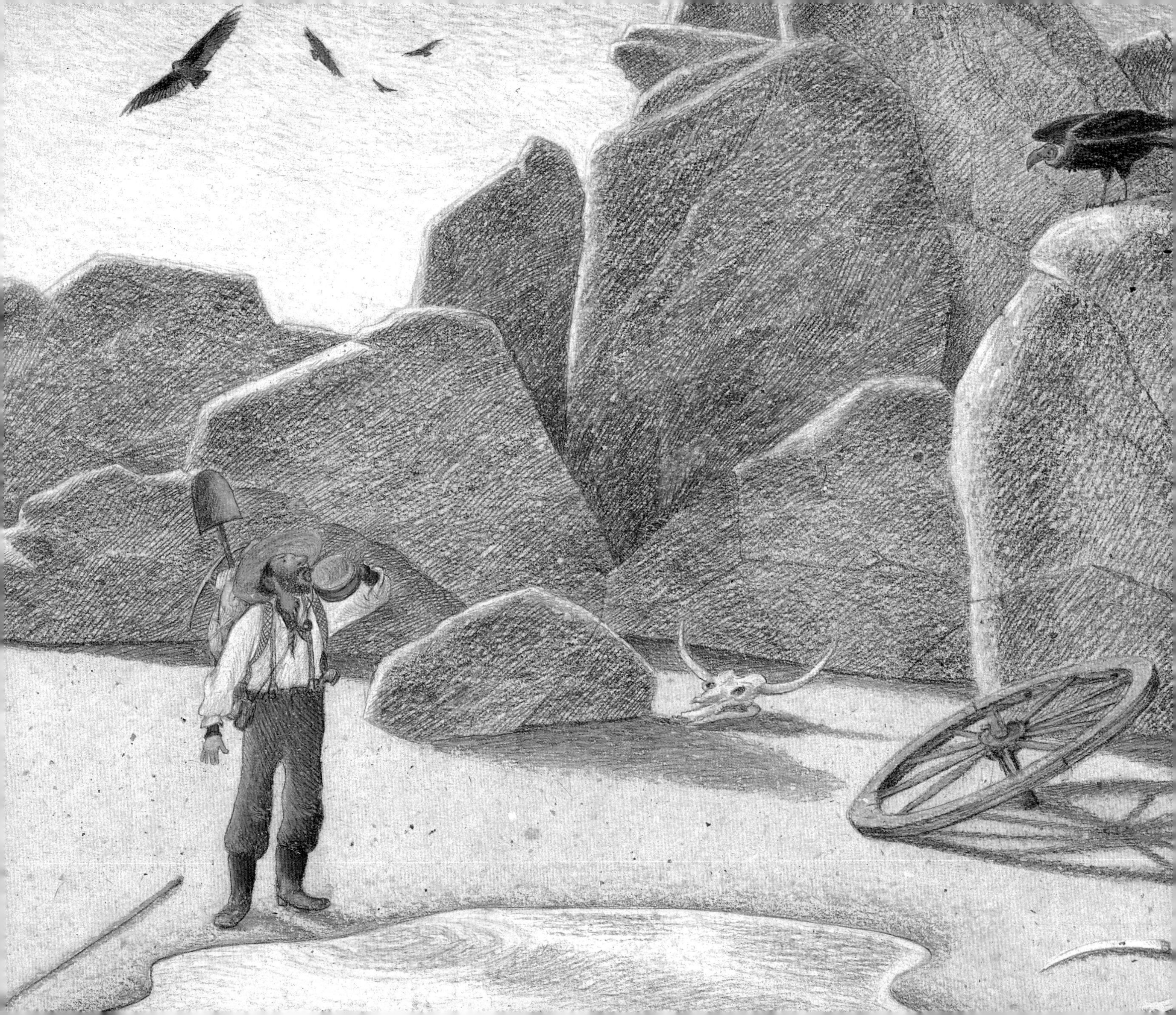

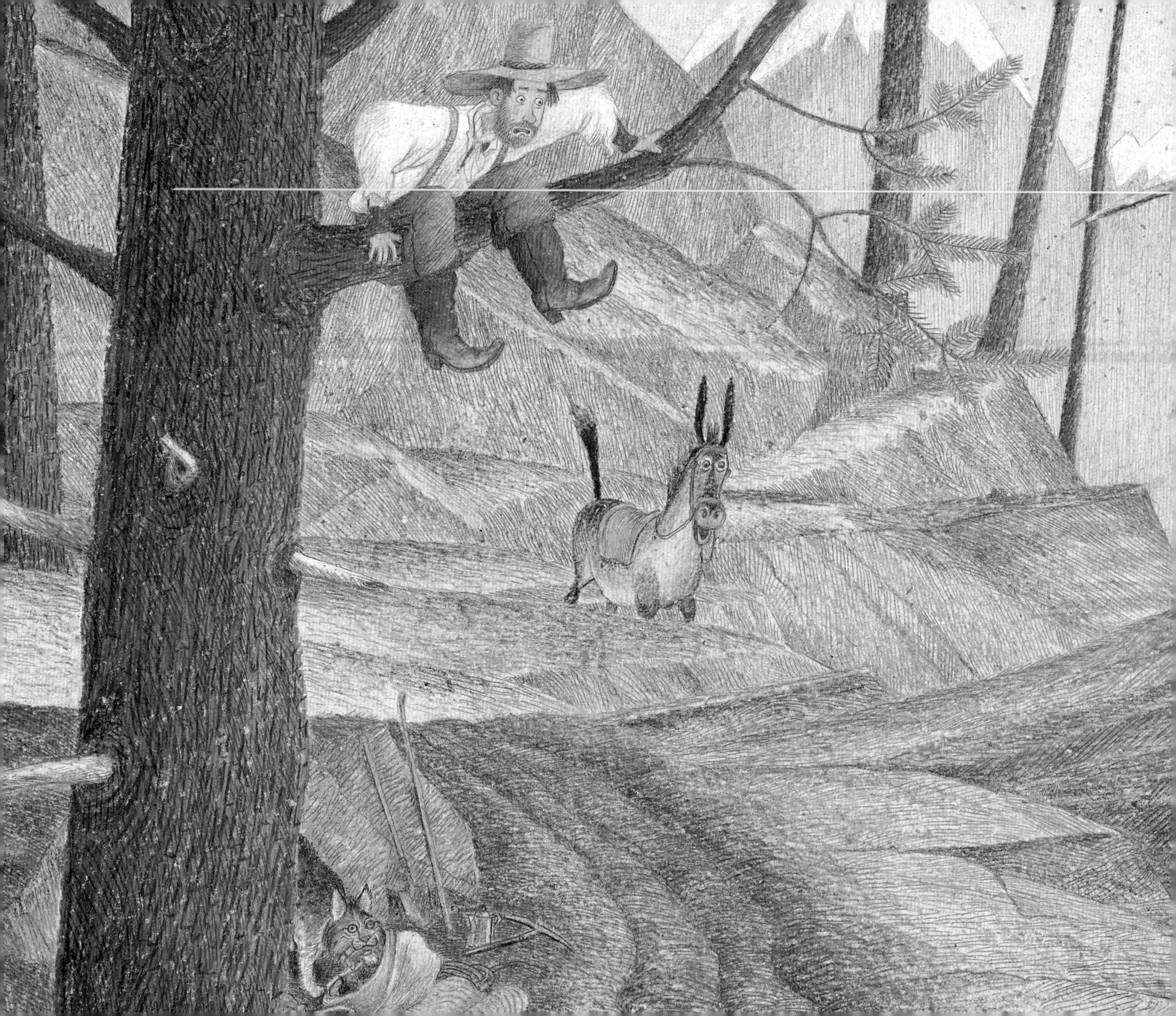

Granite mountain,
Grizzly bear.
Rocky outcrop,
Bobcat's lair.

California,
Gold and green.
Crowded diggings,
Long tom, stream.

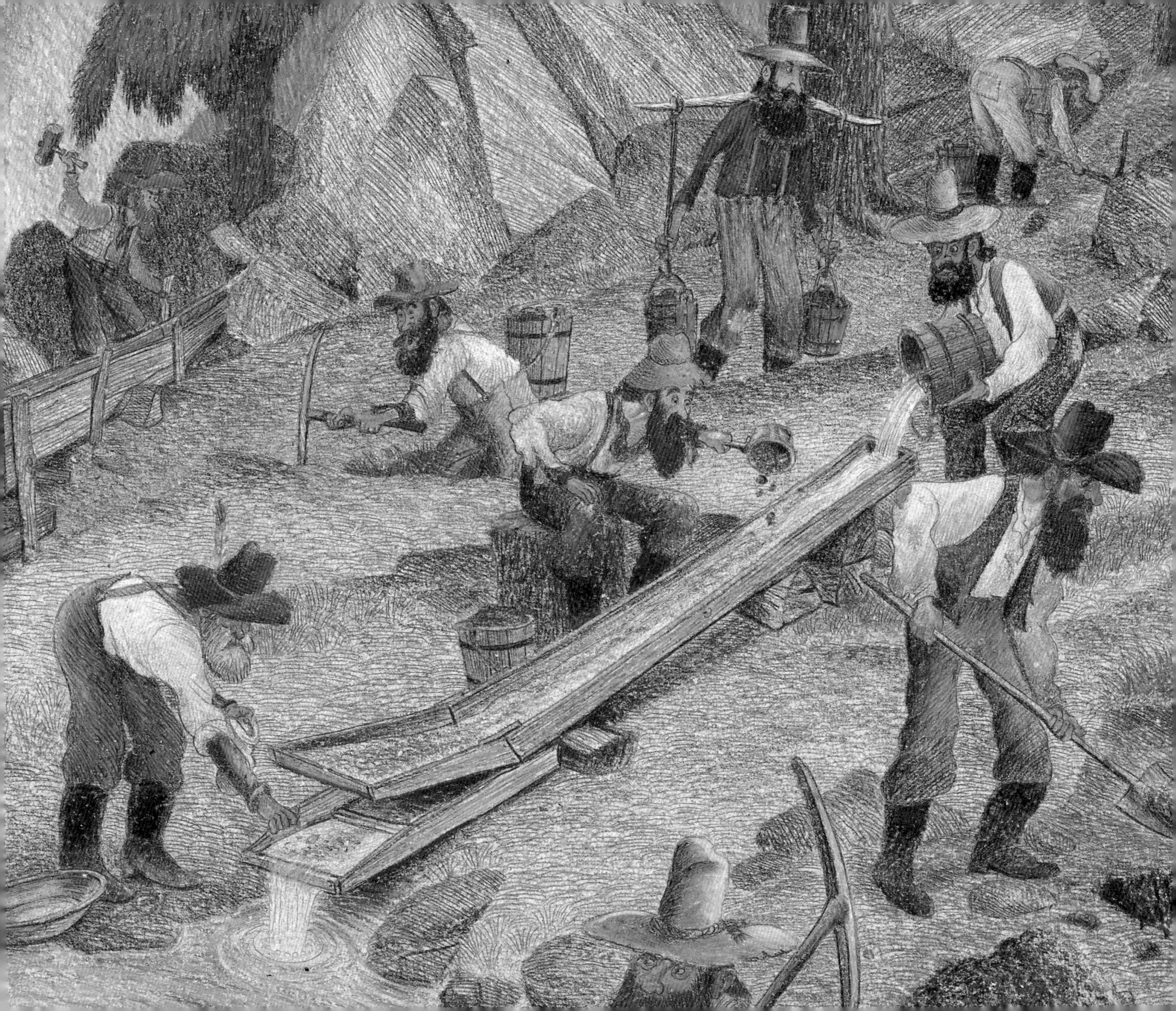

Icy water,
Wet feet, cold.
Sluicing, panning,
"Where's the gold?"

Grumpy miners,
Nuggets—*small*.
Jasper scowling,
Fireside brawl.

Tired, hungry,
Dirty, sore.
Nearby tent-town,
Tavern, store.

Coffee, bacon,
Sugar, beans.
Empty pockets,
Jasper's jeans.

Back to pry bar,
Heavy pails,
Rocker, cradle,
Hammer, nails.

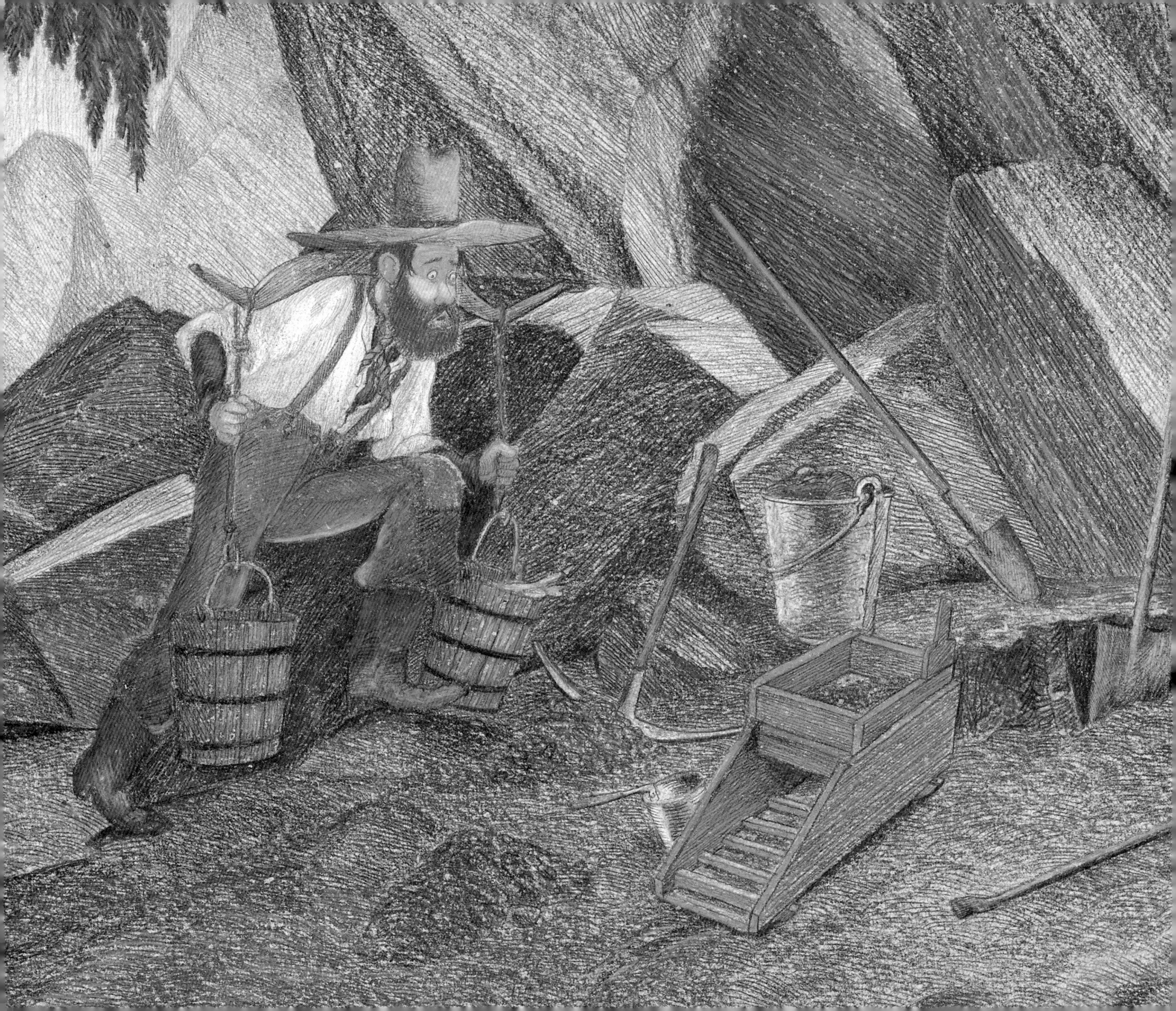

**Busting bedrock,
Boulder rolled.**

Shovel, digging;
"Where's the gold?"

Narrow quartz vein,
Tiny flakes.
Rocky crevice,
"Rattlesnakes!"

Crusty long johns,
Smelly shirt.
Sweat-stained britches
Caked with dirt.

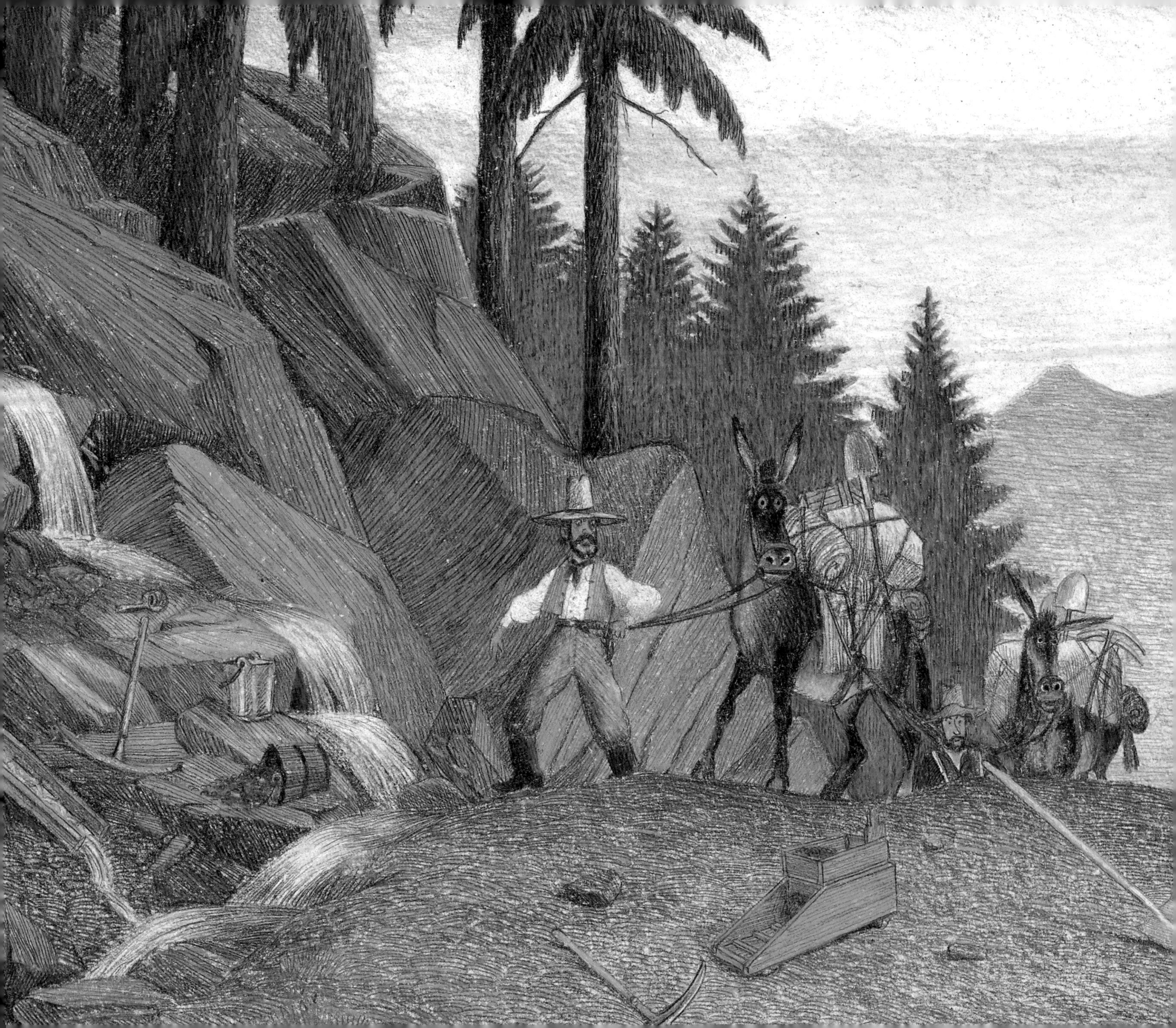

No gold pockets,
No rich vein.
Jasper leaving,
Quitting claim.

Back to farmhouse,
Chickens, cow,
Barnyard, fences,
Pitchfork, plow.

Family waiting,
"Where's the gold?"
Jasper shrugging,
"Warn't like told."

Dashing westward,
Forty-niners.
Jasper waving,
"Good luck, miners."